Arnie the Doughnut

cooked up by Laurie Keller

Henry Holt and Company New York

Downtown Bakery

Home of the Best Doughnuts A - "Round"!

iG CITY

SHOES

ANTIQUES

CLOSED

CLOSED
Why do you need a
Lava lamp at this
hour anyway?

HOURS
6 AM–6 PM

For Cookie and for Sage

Arnie turned out to be just the kind of doughnut he hoped he'd be—

chocolate-covered with **bright**-colored candy sprinkles.

Look at all my SPRINKLES—
there must be a MILLION of them!

ACTUALLY, there are only 135, but I'm not going to spoil it for him.

SPRINKLE INVENTORY
ARNIE
RED 26
YELLOW 26
BLUE 28
PINK 27
GREEN 27
Total 135

Get it? A-ROUND??
We're round.

Give me a minute—I'm good at these.

He was made very early in the morning at the
Downtown Bakery—"Home of the Best Doughnuts A-'Round'!"
Arnie was proud to be one of the best. He knew that people all over town
made special trips to his bakery to buy doughnuts of their very own.

As Arnie sat on the tray, which had just been placed in the doughnut case, he took a moment to reflect on the amazing things that had happened to him that morning.

1. CUT INTO RING

2. DEEP-FRIED

3. COOLED

4. ICED

5. SPRINKLED

6. NAMED

Arnie looked around and saw all sorts of doughnuts sitting nearby.

He tried to strike up a conversation with an apple fritter
on the next tray over, but she didn't seem to want to talk.

"It is rather early. Maybe she's not
a morning doughnut," Arnie supposed.

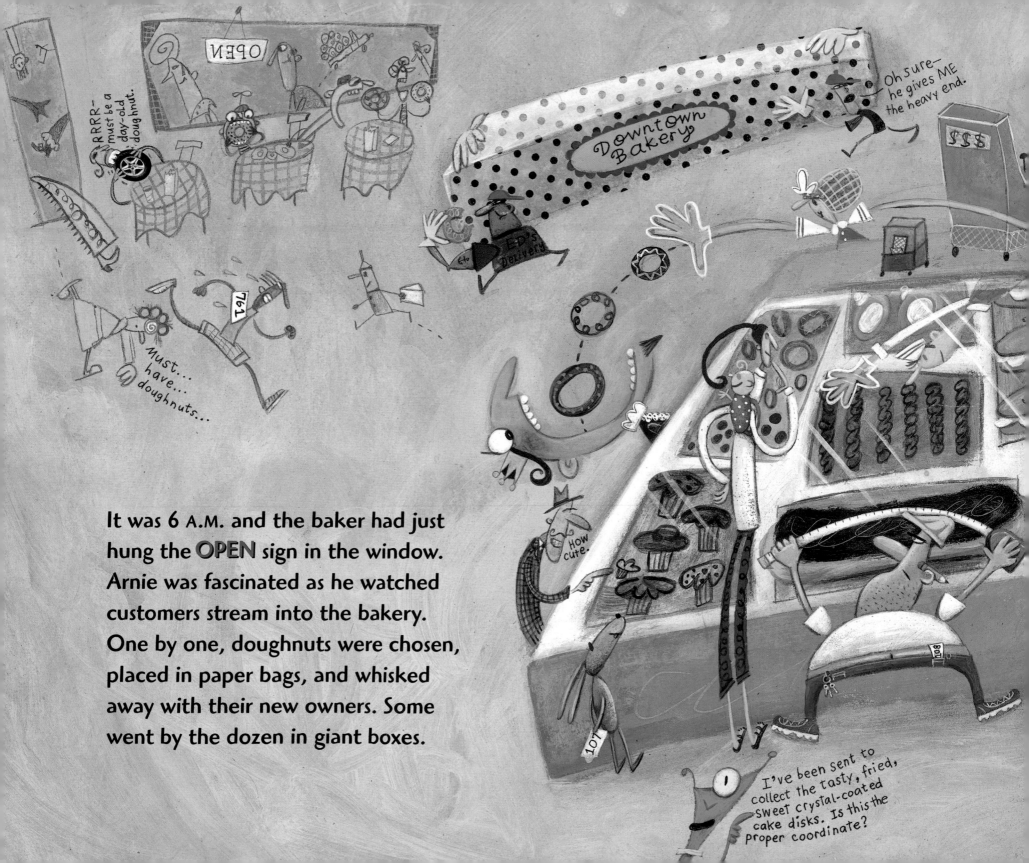

It was 6 A.M. and the baker had just hung the OPEN sign in the window. Arnie was fascinated as he watched customers stream into the bakery. One by one, doughnuts were chosen, placed in paper bags, and whisked away with their new owners. Some went by the dozen in giant boxes.

Just then, Arnie looked up and saw a man pointing right at **him**!

Moi?

"Moi" (pronounced "mwah")
is the French word for "me."
He learned it from moi.

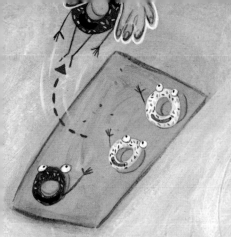

Before he could say another word, he was pulled from
the tray and placed in a paper bag of his *very own*.

Good-bye, everyone!

Downtown Bakery

"Thank you, Mr. Bing. Have a nice day!" Arnie heard
the baker say
to the man.

"Mr. Bing . . . that's
a fine name," Arnie
decided. "I can hardly
wait to meet him!"

GOOD-BYE ARNiE!

We'LL MISS YOU!

Downtown Bakery

ARNiE

I should have talked to him while I had the chance.

(the grand exit that Arnie's imagining)

Downtown Bakery

The ride to Mr. Bing's apartment was a little bumpy.

Arnie was grateful for the soft napkin the baker had so thoughtfully placed underneath him in the bag.

He had never ridden in a car and wished he could look out the window to see all the sights. But more than anything, he wished he could meet Mr. Bing.

"Why does he keep me in this bag?"
Arnie wondered.

Bumps and LUMPS

CLUMPS of BUMPS

thump thump

Finally, the car came to a stop and they were home.

Get those WORDS off my Lawn!

GRUMP on a stump

Mr. Bing carefully removed Arnie from his paper bag and
placed him on a clean, shiny plate.

"What a handsome plate,"

Arnie said to himself.

"I'm not crazy about the design—
I prefer a more modern look.
But it's nothing a little paint
can't fix."

Mr. Bing gently lifted Arnie
from his new plate.

"Isn't that cute?"
thought Arnie, as he closed
his eyes and smiled. "He wants
to hold me."

As Arnie relaxed in Mr. Bing's hand, he felt himself moving higher and higher away from his plate.

When he opened his eyes to see where he was going, he discovered that he was headed straight for Mr. Bing's **OPEN MOUTH!**

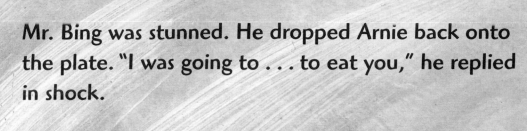

Mr. Bing was stunned. He dropped Arnie back onto the plate. "I was going to . . . to eat you," he replied in shock.

"EAT ME?" Arnie shrieked, his sprinkles flying everywhere. **"Why would you do a thing like *that*? Do you make a habit of eating *all* your houseguests?"**

"Nnnno . . . of course not."

"So, why then did it suddenly occur to you to eat ME?" Arnie demanded.

"Well . . . because . . . you're a *doughnut.* That's what doughnuts are for—to eat."

"Do you mean to tell me you've done this *before*?"

"Yes . . . I eat a doughnut every day," Mr. Bing said sheepishly.

Arnie  froze.

He felt **SICK**

UGGGH.

and **FRIGHTENED**

I'd better get out of here before he tries to eat me again!

and **ANGRY!**

WeLL, that explains why my friends never write or call— they've probably all been **EATEN!**

He thought to himself for a moment. "I must put a stop to this right away! I'll call the bakery and warn the others. Whoever's **LEFT**, that is!"

Arnie knew that there was no time to waste and that he needed to be *very sneaky* in order to keep his plan from Mr. Bing. He turned to Mr. Bing and said in his sweetest voice, "Excuse me, sir, but I don't believe we've been properly introduced. My name is Arnie."

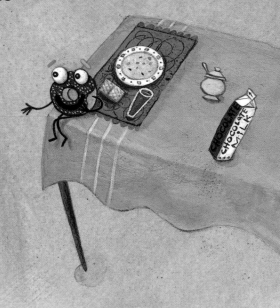

"Um . . . hello . . . Arnie," Mr. Bing stammered. "I'm . . . Mr. Bing. It's nice to eat you— I mean **meet** you."

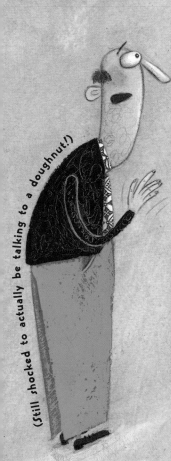

(Still shocked to actually be talking to a doughnut!)

"Mr. Bing, would you be a dear and allow me to use your telephone?" Arnie asked extra politely.

"Oh . . . well . . . okay," said Mr. Bing, and he handed Arnie the phone.

As quickly as he could, Arnie dialed the number of the bakery.

The baker answered the phone.
"Downtown Bakery, home of the best—"

"Mr. Baker Man!" Arnie frantically whispered.
"This is Arnie the doughnut. Do you remember me?
You made me at 5:15 this morning, and I was bought
about twenty minutes ago by a man who goes by the
name of Mr. Bing."

"Yes, Arnie," the baker answered. "What can I do for you?"

"Now, I don't want to alarm you, but just moments
ago, that man tried to eat me! And not only that—
he claims to have eaten hundreds of us!
I'm going to make a run for it, but I
wanted to warn you so that if you
see him coming into the bakery
again, you can **stop** him!"

"Oh my, Arnie—I thought you understood. That's why I make doughnuts . . . for people to **eat.**"

"I CAN'T BELIEVE IT!" Arnie gasped. "Are the other doughnuts aware of this arrangement?"

"Well, I think so," the baker said. "Let me ask them to make sure."

"**Did you hear that, Arnie?**" the baker asked.

Arnie was crushed.

The phone dropped from his hand.

He'd heard all he needed to hear.

Arnie forgot all about his plan to escape. He collapsed back onto the plate, glanced up at Mr. Bing, and muttered,

"All right then, let's get this over with. Go ahead and eat me."

Mr. Bing gazed down at Arnie. "I'm not going to eat you, Arnie," he said reassuringly. "I just wouldn't feel right about it now."

"REALLY?" Arnie said, with a huge sigh of relief. "Well, I'm glad to see that you've come to your senses!"

"But since I'm not going to eat you," Mr. Bing continued, "I'll have to figure out something else to do with you. I paid good money for you— I don't want to be wasteful."

"Of course not!" Arnie agreed.

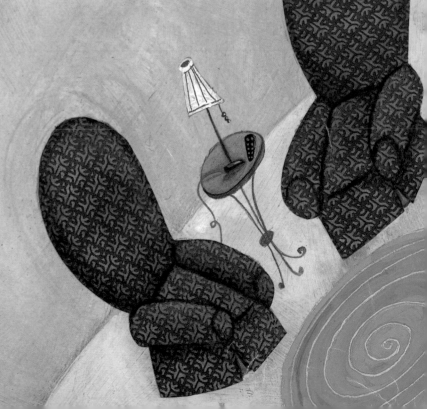

"What we need to do is
each make a list of things
I can do with you instead of
eating you. Between the two
of us, I know we'll come up
with something."

"Good plan, Mr. Bing!" Arnie said. "This
will be a breeze—I bet I'm good at lots of stuff!"

They both feverishly wrote down their ideas.
When they were finished, Mr. Bing asked,
"Would you like to read yours first?"

"Sure thing, Mr. Bing!" Arnie answered.

"Things Mr. Bing Can Do with Me Instead of Eating Me"

"All righty, Mr. Bing. Let's hear what you came up with!"

"Okey-dokey," he replied. "I just know you'll like some of these."

"Things I Can Do with Arnie Instead of Eating Him"

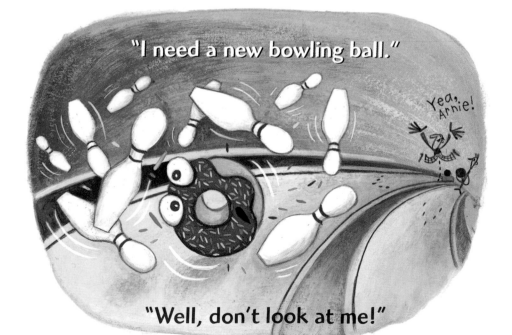

But there was nothing else on Mr. Bing's list. They were both **completely out of ideas.**

Arnie and Mr. Bing were exhausted. They felt terribly disappointed. After a few minutes of awkward silence, Mr. Bing finally spoke.

"I'm sorry, Arnie—but it's clear that we can't agree on anything for you to do around here. This is difficult for me to say, but I think it would be best if you found another home."

"I know," said Arnie, fighting back tears. "I'll just be on my way then. Is it all right if I keep this napkin to pack up all my loose sprinkles?"

"Of course," Mr. Bing replied sadly.

"As soon as I get a job, I'll pay you back the money you spent on me."

"That's not necessary, Arnie."

Good-bye, ARNIE — we've got some lovely parting gifts for you.

Arnie shook Mr. Bing's hand and thanked him for his kindness. Mr. Bing opened the door, and as Arnie left he paused and said,

"I guess doughnuts really *are* only good for eating, aren't they?"

They both waved good-bye and Arnie was gone.

He passed the tennis court, the swimming pool, and the clubhouse.

But when Arnie reached the
NO DOGS ALLOWED
sign at the end of the driveway,
Mr. Bing suddenly came up with
a new idea.

"Arnie! Arnie! Wait up!"

yelled Mr. Bing as he ran after him.

Arnie turned back and stopped. When Mr. Bing caught up with him, he was out of breath.

"I can't believe I didn't think of this earlier!" Mr. Bing panted. "Arnie,

I've always wanted a dog and could never have one because they're not allowed here. But there's no sign that says:

Keep talkin', big guy.

NO DOGS ALLOWED

NO
DOUGHNUTS
ALLOWED."

Arnie perked up when he realized what Mr. Bing was thinking.

"Would you like to take walks and play fetch?"
Mr. Bing asked excitedly.

"You *bet* I would!"

"Can you do tricks, like rolling over?"

"ROLLING OVER?
LOOK AT ME—
I was *MADE* for
rolling over!"

"Well, then, there's only one thing left to ask.
Arnie, will you be my doughnut-dog?"

"Oh, Mr. Bing—
I would **LOVE**
to be your
doughnut-dog!"

NO
DOGS
ALLOWED

It's a WACKY
idea, but it
just might
work!

From that moment on, Arnie and Mr. Bing were inseparable. Arnie liked being a doughnut-dog even better than he liked being a doughnut!

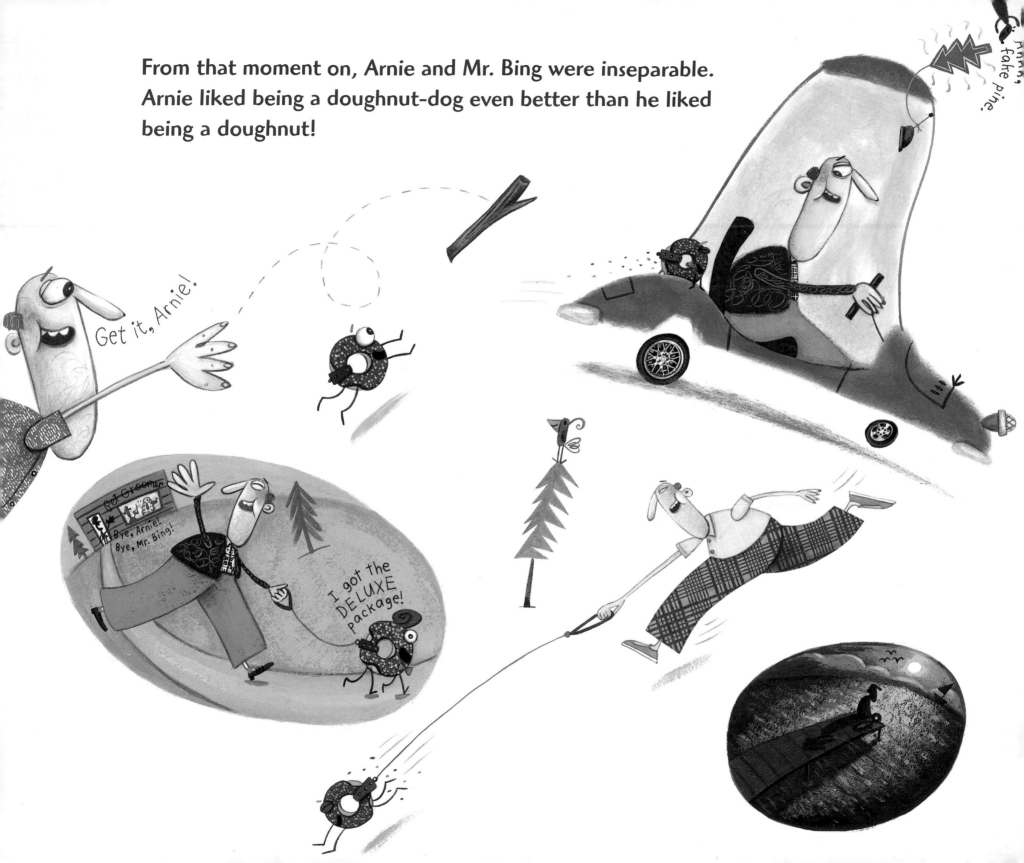

He went through a short phase of chewing on furniture and barking at the mailman, but after a crash course in obedience school, he graduated **first in his class**.

Everywhere the two of them went, people would stop to pet Arnie. No one had ever seen a doughnut-dog before.

Arnie and Mr. Bing had so much fun together.
Arnie was the best pet Mr. Bing could ever have hoped for—
and Mr. Bing was Arnie's best friend.